GOLDEN CHILD

Original script by
Dava Savel
adapted by
Graham Marks

ITV

BOXTREE

First published in the UK 1992
by BOXTREE LIMITED, 36 Tavistock Street, London WC2E 7PB

1 3 5 7 9 10 8 6 4 2
Copyright © 1992 The Walt Disney Company
All rights reserved
1-85283-712-8
Design and illustration by Arkadia.
Printed and bound in Great Britain by Lawrence Allen Ltd., Weston-super-Mare
A catalogue record of this book is available from the British Library.

GOLDEN CHILD

I like the mornings in our house. They're so nice and peaceful, all you can hear is the chomping of food and the switching of channels on the TV. No one talks, except the baby. He talks to the TV because no one talks to him. He particularly likes that science programme, what's it called now...oh yes...'Ask Mr Lizard!' He likes that a lot, especially when that friendly Mr Lizard blows up one of his assistants and has to get another one.

I don't understand it myself, but then I don't really watch the TV, I just shovel food in front of my kids like a good mother should. Mind you, getting that baby to eat can be quite a trial. He only eats what he wants to eat, and you have to watch him like a hawk around the fridge.

Actually, it was not watching around the fridge that was the start of all our troubles. Charlene and Robbie should have been watching the baby, but you know kids - say one thing to shut you up and then do the exact opposite.

Well, my sweet little chutchy went straight into the kitchen and ate everything the fridge gave him; biscuits, sweets, cake, ice cream and a whole bag of sugar. By the time I got downstairs the little darling was having such a glucose rush that he was vibrating like a tuning fork.

Earl, of course, just dumped the baby back in his high-chair and did his 'Don't look at me - I just pass through here on the way to work' act, instead of being a father. Sometimes I wonder what happened to the man I married, I really do.

As I was clearing up the mess the baby had made in the kitchen, I got the standard Earl lecture on our family; 'I told you two kids, but no, you wouldn't listen. Now there's three of them and two of us - we lost three to two.'

He says this so often that I can recite it word perfect. But it's not what he said when the egg first arrived - he was so proud then!

It was just as he was about to go to work that I noticed the bump on the baby's head. I thought that he must've knocked into something, but by the next day things had changed, the bump had grown more than somewhat.

Could too much sugar do that? I didn't know. And when I don't know I go straight to the doctor, just in case he can think of something that'll keep me from worrying. Our doctor is usually quite good at that.

'It was a bump, then a lump and now it's huge,' I said to the doctor. 'What do you think it could be?'

In the doctor's professional opinion it was "a long, gold bony thing with a point."

Robbie, who had come with me, remarked that it looked like a horn, which I have to say it did, and I asked about the sugar thing.

'I eat sugar,' said the doctor, 'but I don't look like a freak of nature!'

Actually, he was about as useful as a bucket with a hole in it. He didn't know what the horn was, he didn't know how it had got there, and to be honest I'm surprised he'd managed to tie his own shoe-laces he knew so little.

6

I'd asked the doctor not to mention the baby's little problem to anyone, which he promised not to do, but when Earl got home that evening he said the news was all over the place. One of his so-called friends had even congratulated him on having a son and a hat rack. Of course my sweet little diddums didn't realise anything was wrong with him, and he even let Robbie and Charlene play hoop-la with him - until I insisted they stop.

Anyway, Earl was in such a mood when he got home. All he could do was shout and look real mad.

'I want that thing off!!' he yelled. 'Saw it off now!!' Well I told him, I said, 'We're not sawing off a piece of our child's head just because you're getting teased at work! That's not a good reason.'

Then my mother wheeled in waving a scroll with a red ribbon tied round it.

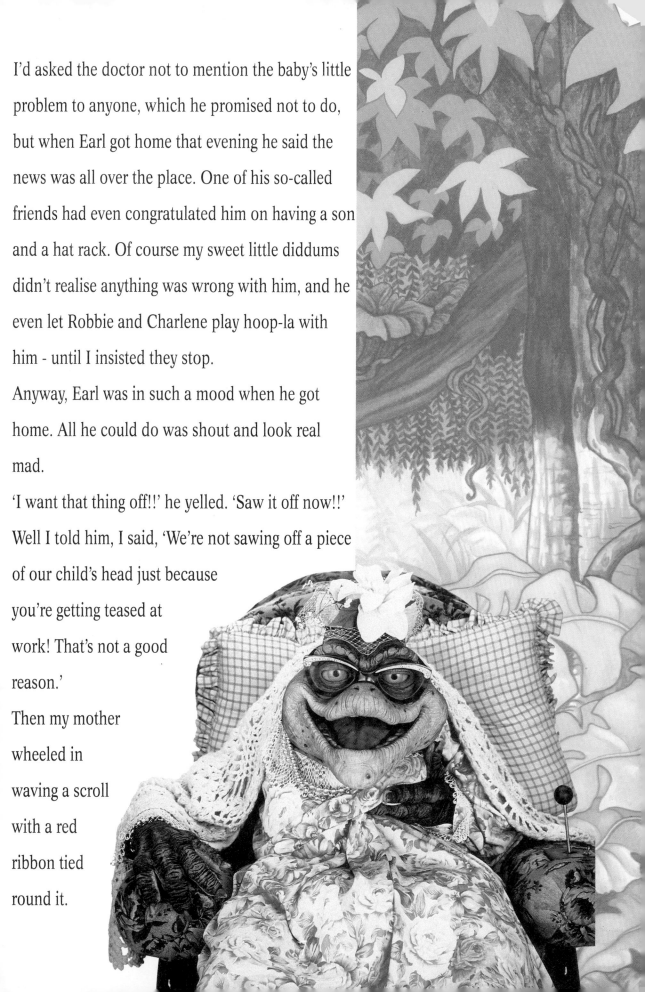

'This, on the other hand,' she said, holding up the scroll, 'is a very good reason!' And I could see from the look on Earl's face that she was right.

Earl wanted to know who had delivered the scroll, and Ethyl told him that it was some dinosaur in a black shroud. That made Earl look even worse.

'It means I've been summoned, doesn't it?' he asked Ethyl, who was, I must admit, smiling rather wickedly.

She told him he was right, he'd been summoned by the Council of Elders, meeting in the Cave of Destiny, deep inside the Mountain of Terror '...that's half a mile from Mort's Big Burger Bar,' she reminded him. 'And they've summoned Earl Sinclair and his infant son!'

All Earl could do was wail 'What have I done? What have I done?' and blame me for having another baby. Robbie brought us all back down to earth. 'What's the big deal about a cave full of old guys?' he asked. He had a point.

I'd heard a lot of silly stories, but Earl obviously believed them. He was beside himself, babbling on about terror and horror. 'I heard they made some guy bite his own head off!' he said, eyes as wide as saucers. I told him to calm down and forget all the mumbo jumbo and rumours.

'This is the modern world!' I told him. 'We don't have voodoo and magic, we have TV and pizza delivery services - there's nothing to worry about!'

Something told me that he didn't believe me. Something else told me that I wouldn't have believed me in his shoes, but there you are. I did my best and made sure they were both very smart when they left the house that night.

Earl and the baby got to the mountain OK and then had to walk down all these dark passages lit only by flaming torches. Why they couldn't run in an electric line I do not know.

Once all the drums and the chanting had stopped, there they were, facing these three hooded ancients. One of them told Earl to put the baby on a big rock and then asked him if he was the father of the child.

'I am,' Earl finally admitted, 'but it's not my fault, honest, I never wanted more than two kids!' He was told to shut up and listen.

It seems the little golden horn was very significant.
One of the hooded ancients read a passage from the
Sacred Book of the Dinosaurs, a very wise book
that I've never got round to looking at.

'And there shall come a child from whom shall
grow a golden horn,' he said. 'And he shall be the
king of the
dinosaurs.'
While all this was
being read out,
Junior had
something to say as
well.

'Gotta go!' he told
Earl. And when he
has to go, he has to
go.
'Hold it in!' hissed
Earl, but it was no
use.

Right in front of all those high up people, and at
such a solemn event, Nature called and a nappy
was filled to the brim there and then. If I'd been
there I would have died.

Well, from there on in things went from silly to absolutely ridiculous. The TV stations went to town, there were reports on the radio and the papers carried blow-by-blow details of the story - thankfully without mentioning the nappy incident.

I have to say that it was very strange to be in the middle of something and watching it on TV as well. After Dinosaur News Network, DNN , had shown what had happened at the Cave of Destiny the night before, they switched to chez nous today, and there was our house surrounded by hordes of people.

In fact, that was how I knew Earl was coming home. I saw him on the television. Very modern.

'According to my sources,' said the DNN reporter, 'the king is holding court at the Sinclair house!'

But to watch him, you'd have sworn it was Earl doing that.

He came wading through that crowd, calling everyone 'peasant', referring
to himself as 'father of the king' and the baby as 'Daddy's little
monarch'. To say that all this had gone to his head would have
been like saying that the sun was a little warm.

He'd insisted that the baby's high chair be re-covered in purple
velvet with gold brocade trim, and he started to call Robbie
and Charlene Prince and Princess. He also had
them organising admissions to see the king.
There was a queue for a mile to get in and Earl
wouldn't send them away even though the baby was
almost asleep in his chair.

'The problems of state never take a nap!' he said. 'Our
little potentate has subjects to receive, disputes to settle -
sports gear to put his name on!'

Earl couldn't see our little baby any more, just one big
cuddly dollar sign.

Even when three of his friends from work came to visit he was suspicious of their motives, wondering why they'd brought presents - would you believe spices, silk and a plastic fire engine? The fire engine was a great success, and I got some lovely cushions out of the silk. And Earl was kind of anxious to get his own back for the dumb remarks that had been made about the baby's horn - before we all knew what it meant - he really made those friends of his sweat.

Actually, if Earl had been a little bit more honest he would have remembered his own words: 'I told you two kids, but no, you wouldn't listen...' but my husband is always a great one for re-writing history.

After everyone had left I was left with the job of clearing up. And what a mess! It looked as if every single soul in Pangaea had trooped through our house! All Earl did was polish the baby's horn, and Robbie and Charlene just counted their takings from selling 'King-on-a-stick' novelties.

Then in walks Roy, that nice Tyrannosaurus who's Earl's best friend. Earl thought that he'd come to see him, but Roy actually wanted to see the baby, which I thought was rather sweet. I was back in the kitchen when Earl came in saying that Roy wanted to talk to the king alone. 'King? Which king?' I said - I still couldn't get used to my baby being royalty, to me he was still my little chutchums.

When I asked Earl why Roy wanted to speak to the baby alone, he said he didn't know - but to wait a second and he'd have a listen at the door. Some friend.

Turns out that Roy thought that my little

sunshine might have mystical powers of a supernatural nature, which is no weirder than thinking he was a king, if you ask me.

Anyway, what he wanted to ask him was to grant him a wish. 'He wants to play the piano!' Earl whispered back to me.'He wants to eat with a fork and get picked for the bowling team - can you believe that!'

I wanted to know how a Tyrannosaurus was going to do those things, 'I mean they're a nice enough species,' I said to Earl, 'but they were at the end of the queue when arms were given out.' 'That's what he's asking the king to do!' said Earl. 'Give him longer arms!'

Earl stayed by the kitchen door and listened to Roy and the baby.

'So,' said Roy, 'can you do the arm thing?'

'Funny arms!' said the baby. 'Like 'em!'

'You do?' smiled Roy.

'Like you!' said the baby, smacking Roy on the nose with his bottle and then putting his arms out for a hug. As Roy went to give him a cuddle he noticed Earl watching.

'You got a great king here, Pally-boy!'

'Yeah, I know,' said Earl. 'Wanna beer?'

Just as they were about to sit down, Robbie walked in with yet another visitor. I had visions of this going on all night, in fact all the rest of my life.

But my vision turned into a nightmare. The visitor was one of the elders from the Cave of Destiny, standing there in my house, wearing his silly black shroud.

The father of the king had on one of his very best stupid grins when he asked, oh-so-politely, 'Can I help you?' Sometimes I think that maybe my mother was right about Earl. He has a talent for being an idiot that has to be seen to be believed.

'I have come for the child,' said the grizzled old thing, all wrapped up in his black sheet. I did what any mother would have done. I stood square in front of my child, blocking the old guy's path and demanded to know what he meant.

'He is king now - he must join us in the Cave of Destiny,' said the old guy, waving his hand about.

'What are you talking about?' I demanded.

'We must train him in the manner of a ruler!' replied the elder.

I got so mad. I have never been madder…well, Earl forgetting our anniversary got me pretty steamed up, but on balance I think I was the most ticked off I've ever been. 'What makes you think my husband and I are going to stand by while you walk out of here with our baby?' I said, hands firmly on my hips. 'Yeah, yeah!' agreed Earl. 'What makes you think that?' I was very proud of him.

'This is what makes me think that,' said the elder, handing Earl another of those stupid scrolls. Why they can't just tell you things I do not know. Anyway, Earl went that funny pale green colour again.

'He who defies the will of the Elders shall be thrown into the Pit of Despair,' he read in a quivering voice, 'and suffer an eternity of unspeakable torment roasting in the fires of absolute misery!'

The baby went.

Our house wasn't the same after that. Without the baby it was too quiet, it was too clean! We were all taking it quite badly, but, surprisingly, Earl was taking it the worst.

Even Robbie's attempts to cheer him up by hitting his dad on the

head exactly like the baby used to, including yelling 'Not the Mama! Not the Mama!' at him, didn't work. Charlene's offer to throw some food at him was no use either.

We were going to have to face up to the fact that family meals just weren't going to be the same any more. Being the mother and father of a king wasn't turning out to be an awful lot of fun - certainly Earl wasn't enjoying it as much as he had to begin with.

When the kids left the dinner table he broke down. I usually hate to see a grown man cry, but I made an exception for Earl because I think he needed to learn a lesson.

I let him wail, I let him moan. I just wanted to hear him say that it was all his fault and that he shouldn't have let those stupid elders take our baby. And when he finally did, I told him that there was only one

thing he could do if he wanted to ever have two sons again.

'You mean have another child?' he said. Can you believe that? I hate to admit this, but my mother may be right about Earl.

'No!' I told him, 'You go straight up to those ridiculous Caves of Destiny and bring the one we've already got right back here!'

Earl was gone a heck of a long time, but apparently when he got to the caves there was quite a queue. His ticket said that he was number 4079. He had to wait sixteen hours while the four thousand and seventy eight other people in front of him got to see the king with their problems.

The guy in front of Earl had a real problem, though. He thought he'd been queueing up for some salami at the delicatessen. Living proof that you should never send a man to do a woman's job.

So then it was Earl's turn. He stepped up to the throne and guess what? The baby recognised him, yelling out 'Not the mama!' when he saw him. Earl was touched.

The guy in the black sheet told him that he only had two minutes with the king, and to hurry up. What a cheek! If I'd been there I would have given that elder a piece of my mind, I can tell you.

So anyway, Earl stepped up to speak to the baby. He told me that he apologised for not being a better father, not spending enough time with his son. I don't know

how much the baby understood, but at least Earl got to say all those things he should have said ages ago.

'Your two minutes are up!' said the elder. 'Touch the horn and go!' Well, Earl touched the horn and it went! Just fell off!! Earl promises that he had absolutely nothing to do with it, and I believe him.

So what can I tell you? With his little golden horn my baby was the king of the dinosaurs...without it my little sweetums was just my little sweetums. Earl came home with the baby, and no one tried to stop him.

The next day we were still on the TV, but this time they were saying that the whole golden horn thing was a set up. There was the DNN announcer blabbering on about a hoax and I don't know what all.

'Well,' said Earl, 'I wouldn't go that far, but I could've told anyone who'd have listened that my baby was no king - a prince among babies, yes! But no king!' You see what I mean about re-writing history?

So now everything's back to normal in the Sinclair household, Robbie and Charlene spend too much time in the bathroom and yell at each other all the time, Earl goes to work and I clear up. Nothing changes - except that Earl now talks to the baby and I don't get the lecture about being outnumbered by the kids any more!